Thumper

Life on the Farm

By Leona Upton Illig

Illustrated by Makenzie Rustin

Publisher's Cataloging-in-Publication Data:

Names: Illig, Leona Upton, author. | Rustin, Makenzie, illustrator.

Title: Thumper, or, life on the farm / by Leona Upton Illig ; illustrated by Makenzie Rustin.

Description: Second edition. | Baltimore, Maryland : Three Villages Media, [2019] | First edition issued by Ride Publishing, 2016. | Audience: Children and adults. | Summary: A revolution is underway and a way of life is disappearing. Growing up on a small farm in Maryland in the 1960s, a boy faces dramatic changes in his family and in the world around him. In the midst of this turmoil, a dog named Thumper barges into his life: an animal with the face of a hound, the legs of a dachshund, and a tail that can't stop wagging. This piece of Americana is for readers of all ages from 9 to 90.-- Publisher.

Identifiers: ISBN: 978-1-7335130-1-2 (print) | 978-1-7335130-8-1 (Ebook)

Subjects: LCSH: Boys--Maryland--Juvenile fiction. | Dogs--Juvenile fiction. | Farms, Small-- Maryland-- Juvenile fiction. | Farm life--Maryland--Juvenile fiction. | Maryland--History--1961-1969-- Fiction. | CYAC: Boys--Fiction. | Dogs--Fiction. | Farms--Maryland--Fiction. | Farm life-- Maryland--Fiction. | Maryland--History--Fiction. | LCGFT: Historical fiction.

Classification: LCC: PZ7.1.I334 T58 2019 | DDC: [E]--dc23

Table of Contents

Dedication

To my family, friends, and all the farmers and neighbors living up and down New Cut Road, without whom this book could not have been written

Chapter One

We always had dogs. The foxhounds came first.

My sisters told me that they were lean and strong, and white and brown and black, and when they leapt up on their hind legs they were taller than a person's head. I have to take their word for it. That was before my time. Their bark was not like anything you had ever heard—a baying that was more like singing, and when you came near their pen they rushed forward, one climbing over the other, trying to lick you through the slats, and altogether making a noise like the string section of an orchestra in full throttle. They were called "Walkers" or "Julys," and their own names were full of mystery—Night Train and Whistler, and Shadrack and Shem, the last being Biblical names—strange because although we kept a Bible in the kitchen, I never saw Dad pick it up.

These dogs had a purpose in life. On Saturday evenings, when the weather was good, my Dad and sisters would load the dogs into the back of the pickup truck and drive over the dirt road back to the woods. When he got to the end of the field, just before the trees began, Dad would open the trunk and the dogs would tumble out and tear into the woods until you couldn't hear them running anymore, even over ground blanketed in twigs and dry leaves. Leaning against the car, smelling the woods, with everything quiet, my sisters said that it was like being alone in the world, with only the stars for company.

Fox hunting was a listening sport. You listened, and you waited, and if you talked at all, you did so in the hushed tones of a minister leading his congregation in prayer. And when the hounds picked up a scent and started crying and their tenors and basses broke through the trees, Dad and the girls would rush up to the edge of the woods. "Whoo-eee," Dad yelled, urging them on.

Sometimes the dogs would gallop through the woods for a long while, losing the scent, catching it, losing it again, until Dad would call them back in with a "Hee-ya, Shadrack, hee-ya!" My sisters said that if they were lucky, they might catch sight of a red fox racing through the underbrush. But for as long as they went hunting, they never caught one. Or killed anything. Fox hunters don't carry guns.

I guess I should say something about my sisters. They are older than I am, and there are two of them. Eileen is my oldest older sister, and Carol is my youngest older sister. They're okay, but hard to figure out. Eileen always has her head buried in books. She keeps carrying on about people named Steinbeck and Hemingway and Fitzgerald. Once, when her library books went missing, she flew around the house like a crazy person. It was fun to watch. Don't ask me why she never looked under my bed.

Unlike Eileen, Carol would usually be outside riding her bike, or swinging on the rope that Dad had tied to the branch of the big sugar maple out front. One time, when she had swung out to the highest point, there was a loud crack— like a branch breaking—and she hopped off that swing faster than a rabbit and sailed into the grass, rolling over and over. That was funny, too. But after the first few times, the element of surprise wore off. The last time it worked she hollered, "If I catch you, Andy, you're going to know it!"

I never found out what "it" was. I guess that was just as well.

Chapter Two

By the time I arrived on the scene, my sisters were pretty much running the show. My job was to keep my head down and learn from example—as if a boy could do that, in a house full of girls.

Also about that time the beagles began to show up. There was one right after the other. I can't remember all of the early ones, but the later ones were hounds with names like Nellie and Susie and Bo. They came in all sizes and colors. These were dogs with a purpose: rabbit dogs. They were like the foxhounds, only on a smaller scale. Where they came from, I don't know. Sometimes my uncles would bring them over, and sometimes Dad would just come home with one in the trunk of the car. Where they all went to, I don't know, either. Some were good rabbit dogs and stayed a while; but others were not and left. I didn't ask any questions.

The most famous of them all was "Hodges Mobutu, Dog of the Nile." Carol named him. She was taking World History in junior high school that year, and she thought it was hilarious. Girls have a strange sense of humor.

Hodges did look something like the Sphinx: sort of inscrutable, with his ears sticking out around a big frown. He had the Sphinx's dignity, that's for sure. But the resemblance ended there. Hodges was a true rabbit hound who knew his business. He was the most professional dog that I ever saw. On the day after Thanksgiving, Mom would make cold turkey sandwiches for us—my Dad, my sisters, and me—and we would load Hodges in the car and head for the woods and let him hunt rabbits. We never had to wait. Dozens of rabbits lived back there, and it didn't take him long to root them out and send them flying out of the brush. Then you would hear Hodges open up and sing! There was nothing better than listening to him race through the snow, the briars crackling as he roared over them and the whole crystal-cold woods echoing with his song.

Hodges was Mom's favorite. I haven't said too much about Mom, but that is probably about right. Mom is just always there. You might as well talk about the sun. The problem with Mom is that, in a family fixated on the outdoors and dogs, she doesn't care for either. She grew up in Westport, in the city, and she likes grass—short, green grass—and that's about it. It's too bad, because on the farm the last thing anybody pays attention to is grass. Except to try to kill it.

But Hodges won her over with feats that defy explanation to this day. All of our dogs lived outside, and Hodges was no exception. In the morning Mom would go out and feed him dog food and any leftovers from supper. One day, while she was emptying scraps into his bowl, she noticed that he had dragged the straw out of his doghouse. Who knows what got into her, but she decided to clean up the mess and put in new straw. She took off her wedding ring and put it on the sill of the garage window, near his doghouse, and got the shovel and started working. She did a good job.

Hours later, when Mom and I were playing dominoes on the kitchen table, she sat up in her chair. "I don't have my ring on," she announced in a voice that normally sent people ducking for cover.

I looked at her hand. "What did you do with it?"

"I don't—oh, gosh, I left it on the window of the garage!"

And we both got up and ran outside as fast as we could.

It was gone.

We searched for an hour. All around the garage, in the dirt, beside the doghouse, in the driveway, everywhere. Nothing. The worst was when Mom decided to go through the new straw in Hodges' doghouse. But we did it—it was me, mostly, picking the straw out and hunting through the spiders—but no ring turned up.

Mom was upset, but we decided to call off the hunt. When the girls came home from school she spilled the story, and this time, with reinforcements, we went back out again.

Hodges was stretched out on his stomach, paws in front, tail in back, sunning himself in front of his house. He didn't get up to greet us, but just stayed where he was, with that serious face of his, not moving an inch. I guess that caught our attention, because at almost the same time we all yelled, "The ring!" It was lying right between his paws, sparkling in the sun, as if he was guarding it. From that moment on Hodges was "golden," as my sisters liked to say.

He had other amazing exploits, including, if you can believe it, finding Carol's junior high class ring in the grass where she had lost it, but his reputation was already solid by that time. Health-wise, he had his episodes. One year he came down with heartworms. We didn't take our dogs to the vet. Dad had a variety of homemade cures that usually worked. Hodges, however, not only earned a trip to see Dr. Fred but came back with a ton of expensive pills. He was so woozy from the medicine that he let my sisters dress him up in ribbons and hats, and somehow he still recovered. In the summer he would get mange—or what we called hot spots—which Dad treated with his special remedy consisting of mostly tar. Mom called it giving him an oil bath. It wasn't dignified, but Hodges never complained, and it always worked.

Life with Hodges was slipping along, nice and easy. But one afternoon, while I was practicing clarinet in my room, I heard a racket downstairs—music and voices that were getting louder with every beat. I ran down the stairs and collided with Mom, who was making a beeline for the bathroom and laughing as hard as I had ever heard her. Dad was sitting in his rocking chair and looking out the window, just shaking his head.

But the main event was my two sisters. They were dancing in the middle of the room, hands together, whirling in a circle, singing at the top of their voices to a song on the record player. It wasn't Hank Williams, either. It was something new, but it was beyond me what all the fuss was about. I watched until Eileen and Carol collapsed on the couch—still singing, if you could call it that.

Dad and I retreated into the kitchen. We got some soda and butter cookies and sat down at the table, proving that at least two people in the house were still in their right minds.

I didn't know it at the time, but our lives changed that day, and not altogether for the good. It's probably not fair.

But I blame it all on those four guys, singing and yelling about "Dizzy Miss Lizzy." Whoever that was.

Chapter Three

Calamities might be too strong a word. Mom tried to explain that what happened was just the vicissitudes of life. Whatever they were, I decided that I could do without them.

Hodges died. When I got off the bus from school, he wasn't waiting outside on his pad, and when I went to look for him all I could see was his tail. He had turned around backwards in his doghouse, and his head was facing the back wall. He wouldn't move, either; wouldn't even acknowledge that I was there.

Dad walked up behind me. It was unusual to see Dad in the yard and not in the field when I got home from school. "It's his time, Hoss. He's had a long life."

"Why won't he look at us?"

Dad took off his ball cap and knelt on the ground beside me. We stared at Hodges' tail for a few minutes. "Well, you know how he is. He probably doesn't want to bother us with it."

And he didn't. The next day he was gone.

Dad didn't go to work in the field that day, and the rest of us stayed home. I don't want to minimize it; there were red eyes and runny noses all around. But on a farm, you see things get born, grow, and die all the time. It's the way things are.

We buried him on the far side of the tobacco barn, where it was private. Dad dug the hole. I brought my clarinet and played "Moon River." It was the only song that I knew all the way through. When it was over, Eileen and Carol made speeches in his honor, and Dad closed the service by saying, "Here lies Hodges Mobutu, Dog of the Nile, and a real good rabbit hound."

Then we all went in and tried to eat lunch. But it was a busted attempt.

In the evening, Carol got the idea of planting some flowers around the grave, so she dug up some four o'clocks and transplanted them. They didn't last. Birds ate them and groundhogs tunneled though them. Later, some oyster shells and speckled stones appeared on the mound. That was Mom's doing. It was more Hodges' style. Dignified.

But that wasn't the end of the vicissitudes. The fact was,

they were just hitting their stride.

A few months later, Carol and I were getting up from supper when Eileen said, "Mom, Dad, I need to talk to you."

I have since learned that when someone uses that tone of voice, and those words, nothing good is going to come after.

By now, Eileen had graduated from high school with honors, and she was working as a secretary for an insurance company on Charles Street. She was a good one, too. She was making enough money to take night classes at the community college, and she wanted to get a teaching degree. But it was a lot of driving back and forth, and a girlfriend living next to the college was looking for a roommate. Eileen wanted to move in with her.

And then Carol got a scholarship for the state university. She'd be moving out, too—living in a college dorm.

Well, you can imagine. Or maybe not. Folks were different back then. If it was possible for Mom and Dad to be proud and happy and sad and worried all at the same time, this was it.

No one in their families had ever gone to college. Neither Mom nor Dad had finished high school. Mom left early to take courses at the Baltimore Business College, and she worked as a PBX operator until she got married and started having us. Dad quit school to work on the farm.

As for leaving home—that was another thing altogether.

Unless you went into the service or got married, it just wasn't done. You might as well have joined the circus.

But Eileen and Carol knew that things were changing. A revolution was afoot, and those four guys—the Lizzy ones— seemed to be the ringleaders. My sisters left home. In less than five months after Hodges died, it was just the three of us. You could hear the quiet.

Chapter Four

My sisters were home for the Labor Day weekend. Dad was working on the cultivator in the shop, getting it ready to put away for fall. We were drinking ice tea around the picnic table, listening to tales of my sisters' adventures in the big world, when Dr. Fred, who was on his rounds from Millersville, pulled into the yard.

"Hello, Mary, is Henry around? I've got something for him to see."

Mom put her glass down and sat upright. "What do you have in there?"

The girls and I looked at one another. It wasn't like Mom to be rude, but before Dr. Fred could answer, Dad had come out of the shop, wiping the oil from his hands with a rag.

They talked for a while, and then Dr. Fred opened the back doors of his van. We could see medical supplies and crates stacked inside. In one of the crates was a dog. He was yellow and rough looking, and he had a stiff, thick, blue plastic collar around his neck.

We gathered around.

"I've had him for a month," Dr. Fred said. "Bobby over in Dicus Mill found him wandering around. He was in pretty bad shape. No one's showed up to claim him. I'm guessing he's about a year old. He wasn't neutered, so I did the operation, but the darn dog tore his stitches out, and I had to patch him up again. This time I put that collar on him so that he can't reach back and get at the stitches. He's on antibiotics and tranquilizers to keep him calm."

"Tranquilizers!" Mom said.

"What's his name?" Dad said.

"Mr. Pickles. I was having a sandwich in the back of the clinic and he ate the pickles right off the plate. Brazen, if you ask me."

I moved forward to get a better look. "What kind of dog is he?"

"Oh, he's mixed. Mostly Labrador retriever, with some other things thrown in."

"Like dachshund," Eileen said. "Or Chihuahua."

"Try bloodhound," Carol said.

"He'll never make it to Westminster with a pink nose."
Eileen frowned.

It was true. Mr. Pickles did seem like a dog that was
made in a factory. He was about three feet long, and his tail
was almost another two feet, making him about five feet
from his nose to the tip of his tail. But he was only about two
feet high and stood on short, powerful legs. The fur around
his neck was medium length, but all over his back it was
short, and some of it was coming out in tufts, like the kind
you see on a lucky rabbit's foot. He had a bald spot on his
elbow where the hair wouldn't grow. He was yellow, but he
was more than yellow: some fur showed white, and some
brown. His ears were immense, like wings. When he tilted
his head backward he looked like a World War I pilot with a
helmet and ear flaps.

But it was his eyes that held you. They were huge and
golden-brown, and they were the happiest eyes I had ever
seen. He might have had a questionable background, but
pure joy gushed out of every part of his body. His strong,
thick tail never stopped wagging, banging like a metronome
against the bars of the crate.

Dr. Fred stepped back. "What do you say, Henry? The
next stop is the pound." Doc sure knew how to turn on the
pressure.

"Well…" Mom said. It was hard to tell whether she was
worried or relieved.

Dad looked at me, the expression on his face hovering somewhere between a frown and a smile. "You like him, Andy?"

I stared at the dog. He beat his tale louder against the crate.

"Yeah."

In a few minutes, Dad was holding the dog's leash in one hand and a bag of medicine in the other, and Doc's van was crunching out of the driveway. But it stopped with a hiccup before it reached the road, and came roaring in reverse back up to us. Dr. Fred stuck his head out the window. "Don't forget to give him both kinds of pills twice a day, morning and night," he yelled over the noise of the motor. "And keep that collar on him. Don't let him get at those stitches. I'll be back in two weeks to see if they're ready to come out. Walk him on the leash and keep him in the house so you can keep that incision clean." The van lurched down the driveway again and onto the road.

We barely heard Mom's voice say, "Keep him *where*?"

Chapter Five

By this time, I had figured out some things on my own. Those vicissitudes, for example. They could be large or small, good or bad, and the only thing that you could count on was this: they showed up anytime they felt like it. You could forget about locking the door.

Mr. Pickles entered the house on probation. Mom found some old bath towels to make a bed for him and installed an accordion-type gate in the doorway between the kitchen and the living room. She made it clear that Mr. Pickles had to stay in the kitchen at all times, until he was able to go live outside. No exceptions.

The first night was the scariest. Except for the next.

That first night, upstairs in our beds, we could hear him pacing the floor below us. My sisters and I knew that if there were any accidents, we would be in for a bad time. Also, if he started howling. But he never made a sound, except for that steady padding around the kitchen. Around eleven o'clock it got quiet, so I went downstairs to check on him. He was lying down with his head on his paws, but when he saw me, he got up and came over to be petted. There were no puddles—or anything worse—on the floor. So far, so good.

When I went back upstairs, I heard Mom talking to Dad, her voice low and soft, from behind their bedroom door. "Getting him a pet is one thing, but why this one? That animal is on tranquilizers! You know who's going to end up taking care of him. And that face of his—he almost looks like a hound dog."

"You really think so?" Dad sounded kind of pleased.

The next day Eileen and Carol and I took turns walking him around the yard. He wanted to jump on us, and he pulled hard on the leash, and it was Carol who said what we were all thinking: "If he's this strong now, what's he going to be like when he's not on tranquilizers?" Carol and I watched as Mr. Pickles dragged Eileen from one end of the backyard to the other. We guessed that he was about seventy pounds. That was more than I weighed.

That evening, after my sisters had left, my Uncle Bill

called to ask Dad for help fixing his car. Dad always dropped everything whenever one of his brothers needed him, so he went out, promising to be back as soon as he could. Mom settled down in the living room to read one of her ladies' magazines, and I started my spelling homework on the floor beside her. Mr. Pickles napped on his towels in the kitchen.

The thunderstorm that came up wasn't that bad. Lots of storms blow through our part of the country, and this one was nothing. But at the first rumble of thunder, Mr. Pickles rose up from his towels and headed for the gate. He had a kind of crazy look in his eyes that said, "I'm coming through."

And he tried. His legs were too short for him to jump over the gate. So I guess he did the only thing, in his mind, that he could do: he stuck his big head through one of the accordion openings and tried to bull his way through the gate. That didn't work, and when he pulled his head back, the accordion gate tightened around his neck like a vise.

Sometimes, when you're watching TV, you see folks yelling, and carrying on, and in general behaving like they've lost their minds. It never hit me until then that I could be one of them. Or Mom.

We rushed the gate. Mr. Pickles pushed through the opening again, this time harder, and the accordion slats loosened. I grabbed his collar and his nose and tried to hold him while Mom yanked the gate out of the doorway. I hadn't ever seen Mom move so fast. I shoved Mr. Pickle's head back through the opening and then the gate and part of the door trim, and Mr. Pickles and Mom and me, all went down with a crash.

Mom was checking my homework when Dad came back later that evening. A pile of door trim and wood strips was neatly stacked on the kitchen floor. I was lying on the couch, watching TV. And Mr. Pickles was lying on top of me, snoring away.

That was how we learned that he was scared of thunderstorms. Or any loud noise, as it turned out. We also found out that he liked to go to sleep at eight o'clock—not seven-thirty, or eight-fifteen, mind you, but eight sharp—and that it was best for all concerned if he started out by napping in somebody's lap. He was one big baby, all seventy pounds of him.

From that time on he had the run of the house. I could be wrong, but I think he set an all-time record for a homeless hound, going from jail to freedom in just two nights. He never did go live outside.

Chapter Six

After a couple of days, I decided that Mr. Pickles was not a good name for him. The whole family tried to come up with a new one. My sisters made fun of his big-baby act and suggested names like Mr. Sweet Pea, Mr. Sweetness and other embarrassing things. We finally settled on Thumper. It was for his tail, which thumped hard against people, cabinets, doors, walls, and anything that was around him when he was happy, which was pretty much all of the time.

As first-time house-dog owners, we were in for some

shocks. After he ate half a pound of butter and a banana—
skin and all—from the kitchen counter, we shut our food
away in cabinets. Sadly, his personal hygiene left a lot to be
desired. I don't know what he was trying to do as he scooted
across the living room rug on his rear end, but it couldn't
have been good. He had no modesty. He would follow you
anywhere, as Eileen found out when she went into the
bathroom to get her hairbrush and left the door open. And I
didn't have to guess what happened when I heard Carol
yelling in the bathtub. Thumper could push most of our
doors open with the brute force of his head and nose.

He had peculiar ideas about socks. He wouldn't steal
them, or chew them, but he didn't want you to put them on.
If you were sitting on the bed, trying to get dressed, he
would roll over on your feet to stop you from putting on
your socks. He seemed to think that he was saving us from a
diabolical sock menace—or something.

In time, the medicine ran out, the stitches came out, and
the medical collar came off, too. His appearance changed: his
ears darkened and got larger. When he flapped them, you
needed to stand clear because they could slap you hard. His
tail grew and filled out and made an even bigger noise
thumping around the house. His coat got thicker and shinier.

But his face was the most singular part of him.
Sometimes he looked like a happy-go-lucky puppy, and
when you talked to him he would cock his head to the side

like he could almost understand you, as if he was saying, "Come again?" At other times, he would hang down his head, his big jowls drooping, and he looked to be about a hundred years old. He was, in turn, either Howdy Doody or President Johnson, depending on his mood, the phase of the moon, your politics, or whatnot. Carol said that he was the chameleon of the dog world. I don't know why. He looked less like a flower than any dog I had ever seen.

The first holidays were memorable, although we did our best to forget them. When Uncle Bill and his family came over for Thanksgiving dinner, Thumper got excited and peed on the kitchen floor—just minutes before we were going to eat. It was hard to know which was worse: the puddle of pee that kept spreading like a pond all over the floor, or the smell of the bleach that Dad used to clean it up. At Christmas I got a new (used) clarinet. Thumper stole the bell and carried it all over the house before I caught him and made him give it up. The teeth marks were impressive. I never told anyone.

When spring came, we found out more about him. He only knew three commands. "Come" and "sit" were two of them. That dog could sit faster than any dog I ever knew. All you had to do was get the "s" out, and his butt went smack on the ground. If there had been an Olympic contest for sitting he would have been a gold medalist. Or a finalist, at least. I don't want to exaggerate.

The third command was "fetch." It was his vocation—his sacred calling—to run down a ball and bring it back to you. And he could do it all day. He was single-minded about it, too. Nothing distracted him. White Fang or Rin-Tin-Tin himself could have showed up, and Thumper wouldn't have given either of them the time of day. Not that he was so good at it. Sometimes he would leap and catch the ball in the air or on the bounce, but most often it would hit the ground and roll, and he would go flying after it. Sometimes he scooped it up on the run, but other times he came up with a mouth full of dirt and grass. One day, while we were playing with him, he missed the ball, slid into the ground, and rolled completely over. Dad turned to me and shook his head. "He's no Brooks Robinson."

He had some habits that were potentially life-threatening, for me and for him. Thumper liked to race around the yard huffing and growling (he never barked), hurtling as close to me as he could without knocking me down, and sometimes even leaping high in the air as he passed me. Eileen called this his wolverine act. Whatever it was, it scared the heck out of me. It took all my willpower to stand completely still when he ran around with that crazed look in his eyes. I had to. Because one false move, to the right or the left, and I might be wolverine meat.

The other thing that we liked to do was run through the tobacco fields. I would holler and throw my arms in the air and run as fast as I could down the rows without touching the sticky leaves, and Thumper would gallop along behind me. But sometimes instead of following me, he would bound sideways across the rows and accidentally break off the leaves. That was a capital offense.

You can believe that it took me some time to patch up the mess. I must have done okay, though, because Dad never said anything to me.

Chapter Seven

Forget what you've heard about tobacco farming.

It wasn't like that. Not on our farm.

Can I tell you about it? I'd like to set the record straight.

Tobacco farming has a rhythm to it; your life gets
tangled in its seasons. So that a fellow might mark out his
life by saying, "Yeah, that happened in planting time," or,
"No, that was in hanging time." Tobacco farming carries you
along, like a river.

Thumper goes crazy with the smells of spring. He

bounds through the just-plowed dirt, ears flying and tail whipping. But he knows to stop when he reaches the tobacco beds. He can't go in there. He sniffs the warm, moist plastic covering the seedlings. In another month those seedlings will grow big enough to be transplanted. Workers will pull them in the morning and plant them in the afternoon.

We are the workers: family, neighbors, friends, and folks who come by needing a job. Dad drives the Allis Chalmers tractor, with a two-seater planter hitched to the back end. As he drives down the row, slow and steady, men on the back of the planter drop the seedlings in the ground. They are working in three-part harmony. Still, sometimes the men will miss a beat. But another fellow walking along behind them will plant a seedling in the empty spot. He plays back-up.

We don't irrigate. On a fifty-acre farm, you depend on rain. But rain or not, the weeds will grow. Sometimes Dad puts me up behind him on the Allis Chalmers while he cultivates. We ride up and down the long rows, the blades digging into the sandy soil, turning it over and cutting up the weeds.

Maryland Catterton tobacco produces deep green leaves in summer that you don't see anywhere else. By mid-summer, pinkish-white flowers burst out on top. Everybody in the family "tops"— snaps off the flowers so that the leaves grow bigger. Suckers creep from the bottom and they have to be cut off, too. Tobacco fights you hard.

But at the end of summer the men cut down the stalks in quick, clean strokes. They let the tobacco lie there, wilting and dying on the ground, for a while. When the men come back they have tobacco sticks with them, cut from poplar at the sawmill, about four feet long. The men spear the stalks with the sharp ends of those sticks, getting six on a stick at a time. Dad hooks the trailer up to the tractor, and the men swing the sticks on top. Defeated, the tobacco heads for the barns.

Those tin-roofed tobacco barns are like ships washed ashore. When the barns are empty, Thumper helps me push the big doors open and we go in. With the side doors closed, it's dark inside, but your eyes get used to it. A big aisle runs down the center, and wooden posts and beams stretch from the floor to the roof on either side. I grab Thumper's collar, and we walk, as stealthily as we can, down the center. If we hear a noise—and you do hear noises, because the wind slips through the cracks and the cypress wood moans—I yell and let go of him, and we tear off toward the far door. The foundation is fine dirt and we kick up a huge dust monster. Mom hollers when she sees us come in the kitchen, gritty from head to foot, my dog and me.

When the rows of side doors are open, the air flows free and sunlight draws patterns on the dirt. The barn changes into a cathedral, with the wind playing the choir. I know some churches that don't have music as good as that.

Well—the workers bring the tobacco in and hang the sticks across the beams. They start with the topmost ones and work their way down until the entire barn is hung with tobacco. The tobacco looks down at you from above and both sides, and it rustles in the air. "I was once a giant," it says, "and now I am hanged." You feel small in that barn.

I can't help with any of this work. But the next job is mine. The side doors have to be opened and closed from the outside to regulate the moisture inside the barn; the right amount cures the tobacco. Even cut from its roots, tobacco cries out for water. Dad uses a stick to unlatch the doors, and I hook them down below. It's a good job, walking with my dog alongside Dad.

Stripping, from October till spring, is the last part. A small stripping room sits off the barn, with electricity for lights and heat so that we can work in the evenings. When the tobacco is dried and brownish-red, it has "come in order" and is carried inside the stripping room. We strip the leaves off the stems, and Dad separates them into grades. He counts out, "Seconds, brights, short brights, tips." It's like he's going up and down the notes of a scale. I'm not good at telling the leaves apart, so I watch. After Dad grades the leaves, he bundles them by taking a bunch of like-graded leaves in one hand, and with his other, twisting a leaf around the end. Then he has what he calls a bundle or a hand.

There are chairs for all of us in the stripping room. Neighbors, and relatives we don't see much, come in and help. You never know who will turn up, and you never know what stories they'll bring. The room is close, the smells are deep, and the talk of the men is low. If the barn is the cathedral, then the stripping room is the confessional.

When the tobacco is stripped, graded, and handed, the bundles are packed and tied between two basket lids, four feet square, one on top and one on bottom. In April, they're loaded onto trucks and travel down the highway to the auction at Upper Marlboro. In a sprawling warehouse the size of two gymnasiums, farmers sell and dealers buy. In a few minutes the tobacco is auctioned off, Dad is paid his money, and we start the cycle again.

Over and over again, except for the year when we didn't.

Chapter Eight

All our supper dishes had been cleared off the table, but Thumper was still in the kitchen, working hard on his "birthday bowl." He had just turned four, at least as far as we could figure. Mom had made a special dinner for him, and he was determined to get the last morsel of chicken out of his dog dish. The rest of us were in the living room reading the newspaper, when Dad looked up from his sports section and said, "We're not planting tobacco next year."

When you do something all your life—and one day you find out that it's been a bad thing all along—I don't know. It must hurt your heart, like finding out that your team's been cheating from opening day. I guess that's how Dad felt. But I don't know. All he said was that the government men had decided that tobacco made you sick, and that it was time to grow something else.

It was too bad. It was a beautiful plant.

But tobacco was done, and truck crops sprouted in its place. They had names that made you want to sing them out: Silver Queen corn, Long John cantaloupes, Jubilee watermelons, Connecticut Field pumpkins, Big Boy tomatoes. We had "sweep-potatoes," too, and it took all our efforts to keep Thumper from grabbing the reddish-orange potatoes and running around the yard with them in his mouth.

We did okay with these new crops, and it was interesting to watch the folks who came to buy them. The local grocery store would send a truck to load up the vegetables and haul them away, but we always had enough left over to sell to people at the house, too. I liked to sit on top of the trailer while customers would tap on the watermelons to find the ripest ones. Thumper would sniff at their feet and entertain the little kids that showed up.

But it wasn't the same. A few years after we started growing vegetables, Dad stopped spending so much time in the field. He'd come home at lunchtime and take a nap, and sometimes he didn't go back out. Uncle Joe, another one of Dad's brothers, began to come over and help out.

When I came home from school Dad might be in his rocking chair, reading. He always had a couple of foxhunting magazines around. Mostly they had pictures of dogs, with white numbers painted on them, standing on benches, looking bored; but they had stories in them, too. He told me about one of them. It was about an old hunter being called home. I never understood it. If that hunter was being called home, why didn't he just go? Dad read a lot of books that my sisters brought home, too—books with titles like *Buff: A Collie*. Dad took to quoting from them, and for one whole week he kept saying, "Heroism consists in hanging on, one minute longer." I never knew what it all meant.

My sisters brought him a ton of baseball books. Dad read them all. He was pretty hard on the current players. Said that some of them were too lazy to run out the balls. Dad had wanted to be a baseball player. But after he quit school to work on the farm, the war came, and he never got around to it. I guess that he would have been pretty good.

One time, when the doctor was downstairs with Dad and Mom, I heard my sisters talking in Eileen's room. Eileen was saying something about Dad being kicked by a mule in the Army, and Carol was talking about rheumatic fever. Then they got real quiet. I couldn't hear any more.

When Dad went to the hospital that winter, he stayed a long time. For a while he was in the veterans' hospital at the old Army site at Fort Howard. Sometimes Mom and I took the bus to the hospital, but it was a long trip. You had to catch two buses, and you could get plenty cold waiting for the bus to come. Sometimes Eileen or Carol would drive us, sometimes relatives would. We had just gotten that routine figured out when Dad was transferred to the veterans' hospital in Washington, D.C. That was a big deal. Mom decided that she was going to learn how to drive out there, and she did (although at first we drove right down the streets and missed all the red lights. Who would have thought those politicians would put them on the roadsides?). So now we had Mom, Eileen, Carol, and a whole lot of relatives driving. It was a regular caravan heading out there every weekend.

It's a funny thing about hospitals. If they're supposed to make you feel better, why does everybody hate to go to them? And why does everyone in them look so serious? Just once I'd like to go into a hospital and find, maybe, a friendly guy sitting at the front door telling stories. And if that didn't work, they could have nice lady inside handing out ice cream cones. I bet that would cheer folks up.

Dad had a lot of relatives and a lot of friends. They all came around, to both the house and the hospital. But I noticed something puzzling about a lot of them. They seemed to think that Dad's being sick was a "terrible burden," and they kept saying how sorry they were for us. But Mom and Eileen and Carol and I never felt that way.

Each day that Dad was with us was one more day that we could take care of him and try to make him feel better. Heck—some kids don't have any mother or father *at all*.

After the operation, they let us take Dad home. The doctors were real nice and gave us lots of instructions. I guess they figured that it was their job, but we never could sort it all out. Dad could still go up and down the stairs, but Mom made up a bed for him on the sofa so he could watch TV and get to the kitchen easier. We didn't have a downstairs bathroom, but we made out okay. I guess the less said about that, the better.

Thumper was real happy when he found Dad sleeping on the sofa. I guess he thought that Dad was sleeping there so that he could have more time to play with him. At any rate, Thumper took to sleeping by the sofa instead of in his own bed. Sometimes he would just sit there and watch Dad, or put his paw on his arm. Thumper's toenails could be sharp, but Dad never complained.

My sisters came home almost every weekend now, and we would all watch the Orioles. Dad would sit in the living room rocker with Thumper beside him. Sometimes they both fell asleep during the game. The sound of the two of them snoring was almost enough to drown out the announcer.

Dad made it a point to get outdoors to look at his vegetable garden every day. And in the evening Dad and

Thumper and I would sit outside in the backyard. When it got dark, he would point out the stars and show me how to tell north and south. One evening, after he had finished drawing a constellation on the ground with his walking stick, he said, "What do you want to be when you grow up, Andy?"

I told him that I wanted to be a bandleader. Or an astronaut.

He laughed. "Well, whatever you do, make sure that you do a good job."

Dad wasn't an old man, but twilight was falling, and I understood.

Chapter Nine

By the time I jumped off the school bus I could smell rain in the air. I ran up the driveway and into the house, and Mom was sitting on a chair next to Dad. He was lying on the sofa and his eyes were closed. I could hear him breathing. He was working hard at it. Thumper was sitting beside them, thumping his tail. It looked like Mom hadn't moved since I'd left that morning. She took my hand as I stood beside her.

"How was school today?"

"Okay. Has Dad woken up?"

"No. I called the doctor. He's coming, but he's worried

about the storm, and he could be late. He heard that the hurricane might head up the Bay. Is it windy out there?"

I shook my head. All I knew was that the storm, the first one of the fall hurricane season, had been off the Outer Banks two days ago. The weatherman had said that it would likely go out to sea, but if it came ashore, it would probably hit New England, if it hit anything at all.

"Sit here with Dad while I get us something to eat. Pull the table over so you can do your homework."

We ate toasted cheese sandwiches while I worked on my arithmetic. I was doing long division problems when the rain started falling. It wasn't much at first. But it got going in solid, steady sheets, and soon it was so dark outside that Mom put the lights on.

It was only four o'clock.

Thumper was restless. At first he kept raising his head, cocking it to one side, like he was listening for something; but afterwards, he took to walking around the house. We watched as he sniffed the air blowing under the window sash.

"I'll get flashlights in case the electricity goes out," Mom said. "Stay here by Dad. If the phone rings, answer it and tell them I'm coming. Yell if you need me."

When Mom got back she had collected four flashlights and an old, wrinkled brown bag filled with batteries. Dad never liked candles. He said we were more likely to burn the house down than produce any light. Mom always drew the curtains at night, and I helped her with the ones in the living room. It was black outside.

Mom tried to phone my sisters, but all she got were busy signals.

The electricity went out a few minutes later. We turned on our flashlights, but their beams didn't do much to cut the darkness. Thumper sat down and watched the patterns the flashlights threw on the wall; he seemed fascinated by the lights and shadows.

On television shows, or in the movies, when big things are about to happen, you always know it. The music swells, or it gets deeper. In real life, some people say that time stops, and you see your whole life going on in front of you, only in slow motion.

But that wasn't how it was with us.

All I can remember is that I was stuck on a problem and needed to ask Mom about where to put the decimal point, and that when I looked over at her, she had her head in her hands. Dad was—still.

I couldn't swallow. I don't know why I needed to. But I felt like if I didn't, I would stop breathing, too.

Mom tucked the blanket up by Dad's head. "It's over, Andrew." She made as if to get up, but I held her arm.

"We can't leave him alone, Mom."

A surprised look filled her eyes and she said, "We won't

leave him. We'll stay right here until the doctor comes." Her voice sounded a long way off.

I don't know how long we sat there.

I remember that Mom went into the kitchen and brought back two glasses of orange juice. The glass felt heavy, and I had to hold it with both hands to keep from spilling it. But when I drank some of it and felt the coldness in my throat, I knew that I could swallow, and I felt quieter inside. I wondered if Mom felt the same way as we sat there in the darkness, listening to the rain, sipping the cold juice.

When the wind started up, it was quick and the roof groaned—the wind swept through the windows into the house and the rain washed like waves over the house. Thumper tried to climb up on my lap but I pushed him down. He tried again when something banged against the side of the house and the back door blew open. He spun and bolted through the open door into the yard.

I screamed and ran out after him. I couldn't see in the blackness roaring around me, and I tripped and fell on my knees. The ground was covered in broken tree limbs and water and mud, and the noise of the plunging branches above me was like a hundred saws. I swung my flashlight around and saw Thumper in the driveway and hollered and he stopped in mid-flight. I half-crawled, half-ran until I caught him and buried my hands in his collar. Mom was running behind me, and when she grabbed my belt all three of us went down in the mud. We were still there when we heard the crack—a sharp report like a gun—and turned to see the big sugar maple split apart and come down on the roof.

After that, I don't remember a whole lot.

I know that the rain let up. It wasn't cold, but I was shivering. I could feel Mom's arms around me and I could smell Thumper's wet fur beside me. I still had hold of his collar. The wind was dying down, too. When I looked up, I could see stars beginning to show in the sky.

If only it was yesterday. If only I could get back *there*.

Chapter Ten

It wasn't long after the night of the hurricane that we moved to town with some of my Mom's family.

A lot of people came around to visit after Dad died. But in a few weeks, the crowd began to thin out, and it was just us and Thumper again. I wasn't sorry to see them go. They talked a lot about Heaven, and how Dad was in a Better Place, and how it was "all for the best," and stuff like that. They usually did this talking in the living room. Mom and my sisters would be sitting on the sofa, listening, hands resting in their laps. But I saw something in their eyes that the rest of that crowd never did: a kind of anger, and a hardness, and I worried that the crowd might be in store for something they hadn't counted on. But I didn't have to worry. No matter how religious those folks got worked up to be, Mom and the girls sat quietly and took it. They had backbone.

As for me, I don't know if I buy all that Heaven stuff. But I don't think it matters. Dad isn't gone—I have him here in my heart.

I should mention that Dad didn't go without controversy, which, knowing Dad, I guess we should have expected. It turned out that he told Mom, after he got sick the last time, that when he took the train out he didn't want a big fuss. And no funeral. He wanted to be cremated, in private. So that's what we did. Judging from the reaction of the relatives, you might have thought that we had stashed him away in the sweep-potato house. Dad was the first in the family to be cremated, and the relatives kicked up such an uproar that for a while it looked like he might be the last, too. But I don't know. I could see that Mom was flat-out determined to do things her way. In any case, it didn't bother me.

After the storm, we had cleaned up most of the broken glass, plaster, and rain-soaked furniture. It was harder for us to see the damage to the roof and sides of the house. Some men dressed all up in suits came to look at it, and they walked around it, and asked questions, and wrote down things in thick black notebooks. In the end, they sent us a letter saying that it wasn't safe to live there anymore, and that we had to move out. It was a certified letter.

That farmhouse had stood for a hundred years. It took less than three weeks for those fellows to kill it.

The first plan was for us to go to some of Dad's relations in south county, but they said that they couldn't take another dog. To which Mom told them, "If Thumper doesn't come, we don't come." I should say right here that Mom had gotten the idea that Big Thump was a hero for getting us out of the house before the tree hit. And nobody was going to tell her differently. So, we packed up and went to live with Mom's relatives instead. They had a house in town, and I didn't have to ride the bus to school anymore. Also, we were closer to Eileen and Carol.

When our new neighbors heard about what had happened, a lady down the street offered to give me clarinet lessons for free. For some reason this got everybody riled up. There was a lot of to-do about "charity cases" and whatnot, until my Mom finally gave in. But I could tell that she wasn't happy. Later on, I heard that she paid the lady anyway.

We kept the farm, and Uncle Joe worked it for us, sharing the costs and the income. Mom got a part-time job at one of the ice cream stores in town, and for years we only had chocolate, strawberry, or vanilla ice cream for dessert. I guess that's why pie tastes so good to me now.

Mom and my sisters and Thumper and I spent a lot of

weekends out on the farm, taking walks, eating sandwiches and drinking ice tea at the picnic table. Somehow the old table had survived the storm. The barns made it through okay, too. But as time went by the house began to sag, and weeds took over the garden. I wasn't there when the bulldozers came in to haul the mess away. Mom wasn't, either. She said that we had seen enough.

Thumper lived to be an old dog. On account of his heroism during the hurricane, he was always the center of attention and the most spoiled canine that I ever saw. My sisters slipped him treats that were more suited for people than for dogs, and Mom cooked hamburgers for him, which was going a little overboard, if you ask me. Some dogs might have gotten spoiled with all the attention. But not Thumper. When that grin started spreading over his face, you knew that he was plotting his next adventure.

That's how Thumper got to be the most famous of all of our dogs. Did he really try to save us, or had he just been afraid of the storm?

I guess only he knows.

And that's okay with me.

Acknowledgments

I would like to thank everyone at 1st Ride Publishing; they produced the first edition and provided invaluable help and advice. A special thank-you goes to Makenzie Rustin, who provided the beautiful illustrations. As always, I want to thank my teachers at Richard Henry Lee Elementary School, Corkran Middle School, Glen Burnie High School, Anne Arundel Community College, and the University of Maryland, College Park, for their support and encouragement.

Finally, many thanks to my family, without whose help, inspiration, and encouragement this book would not have been possible.

The quote on page 42, "Heroism consists in hanging on, one minute longer," is from the novel *Buff: A Collie*, by Albert Payson Terhune, published in 1921.

About the Author

 Leona Upton Illig's fiction has been published by magazines such as *The MacGuffin*, *The North Atlantic Review*, *The Western Online*, and *The Thoughtful Dog*, while her non-fiction has been published by *Sky & Telescope*, the premier astronomy magazine in the United States. As a book critic for Children's Literature, LLC, her book reviews were distributed to libraries and schools around the nation. She has lived in Thailand, as well as in the Middle East, and has developed a deep appreciation for the customs and cultures of other countries.

She holds an Associate Degree in Elementary Education from Anne Arundel Community College and a Master's Degree in English Literature from the University of Maryland, College Park. A member of The Society of Children's Book Writers and Illustrators, the Maryland Writers' Association, and the Eastern Shore Writers' Association, she lives between Baltimore and Annapolis with her husband, David, and a small spaniel named Clara. Further details can be found at her website, http://www.threevillagesmedia.wordpress.com.